THE DRAGONS' INN

Written by
BRUCE DONNELLY

Illustrated by
EVA TUCCONI

To our dearest family and friends for
your love and support - Thank you.

———————————————————

Published by Lost Boy Productions LLC

222 Broadway, Floor 19
New York, NY 10038
USA

Title: The Dragons' Inn / Bruce Donnelly and Eva Tucconi
Names: Donnelly, Bruce, author. | Tucconi, Eva, illustrator.
Identifiers: ISBN 9798986494203 (hardcover) ISBN 9798986494227 (paperback)
ISBN 9798986494210 (EPUB)
Subjects: LCGFT: Picture books.

Library of Congress Control Number: 2022911788

Printed and bound in the United States

LOST BOY
PRODUCTIONS

www.lostboynyc.com

On a **cold** mountaintop, through the deep snow and mist,
there's a place **just for dragons** that is said to exist.

For dragons, you see, also need the odd break,
when they're tired and grumpy and their bodies just **ache**
from guarding *great* treasures or getting into *fights*
with greedy little goblins, ogres and knights.

What they want *most* of all is a place of their own,
to **escape** from this world and be left *all alone.*

So, when the day ends, they *take off* in flight,
to journey to this place *out of reach, out of sight.*
Upwards they climb to where the air is thin,
up to a place called **The Dragons' Inn.**

The inn stands alone on these craggy mountain peaks
and in the cold, howling wind it groans and it creaks.
The dragons arrive one by one through the storm,
to gather inside where it's **cozy** and **warm**.

WELCOME **ALL** DRAGONS
TO THE END OF YOUR QUEST

YOU'VE TRAVELED FAR AND WIDE
NOW COME IN AND REST.

IF YOU'RE HERE FOR A FEAST
OR A LARGE COMFY BED

WHATEVER YOUR BUSINESS JUST
MIND YOUR HEAD!

Now, because dragons come in *every* shape and size,
when they first built the inn they thought it wise
to leave enough room between the ceilings and floors,
to get *every* dragon to fit through the doors.

From the tables and chairs to the windows and beams,
every inch of this place is BIGGER it seems.
With *many* more secrets and spaces to hide,
in tunnels and cellars dug deep down inside.

The **great hall** is filled with tales being told
of *heroes* and *villains* and *legends* of old.
There's music and singing and games being played,
and merchants with **magic and treasures** to trade.

While over in the corner, there are some who desire to sit and do **nothing** by a ROARING great fire.

Climbing on the counter to stand above the crowd,
    the little old innkeeper YELLS out loud:
"I know you're all hungry and ready for some treats.
I'm coming for your orders, so *stay in your seats!*"

With news of the feast, they give out a **_great_ roar**,
for there's **_nothing_** in the world these dragons love more
than sinking their teeth into a big, greasy dish
of juicy red meat or freshly caught fish.

"For starters you can order a bowl of *mice*,
DELICIOUS on their own, or with a side of rice.
While for those of you wishing to try something *new*,
our catch of the day is **rat tail** stew.

Next, you'll be wanting even tastier meat,
in which case you're in for a very **BIG** treat.
Just for tonight you're all in luck,
we have *crackling* **pig** and *Peking* **duck**."

With their mouths hanging open and *covered* in drool
and the one *SO* hungry he *falls* from his stool,

she takes all their orders in a little notebook,
turns on her tail and heads *straight* to the cook.

In the kitchen, the cook stands *SHARPENING* his blade,
while the innkeeper reads out the list she's made.
"...then it's **thirty-six** rats with a starter of snails,
twelve pork pies and fried fish tails..."

With the orders all in, the cook *fires* up the coals
and lines up all of his plates and bowls.
Then he lets out a flame in one **GREAT, BIG** puff,
searing the steaks so they're *just* black enough.

CHOMPING through dinner with their *teeth* and *claws,*
with gravy and grease smothered *all around* their jaws,

the dragons are one **very satisfied** lot,
cleaning *every* last plate, *every* pan and pot.

With the kitchen now *closed* and the dragons all lazy
and all about the room feeling *heavy and hazy*,
the innkeeper **cries:** *"It's time now for bed.
Your bellies are all full and your eyes deep red."*

Huffing and *puffing* they rise from their chairs,
climbing to their rooms at the top of the stairs,
leaving everything calm and bathed in the glow
of the slow-dying fires and the falling, white snow.

Soon all the dragons are **snoring** in their sleep,
while all throughout the inn one can barely hear a *peep,*
but for the **squeaks** of the fortunate few,
who *escaped* from the grill or being *thrown* in the stew.

The dragons wake early as the sun starts to rise
and gather their things as they take to the *skies*.
A **new** day's adventure is about to begin,
before returning once more to **The Dragons' Inn**.

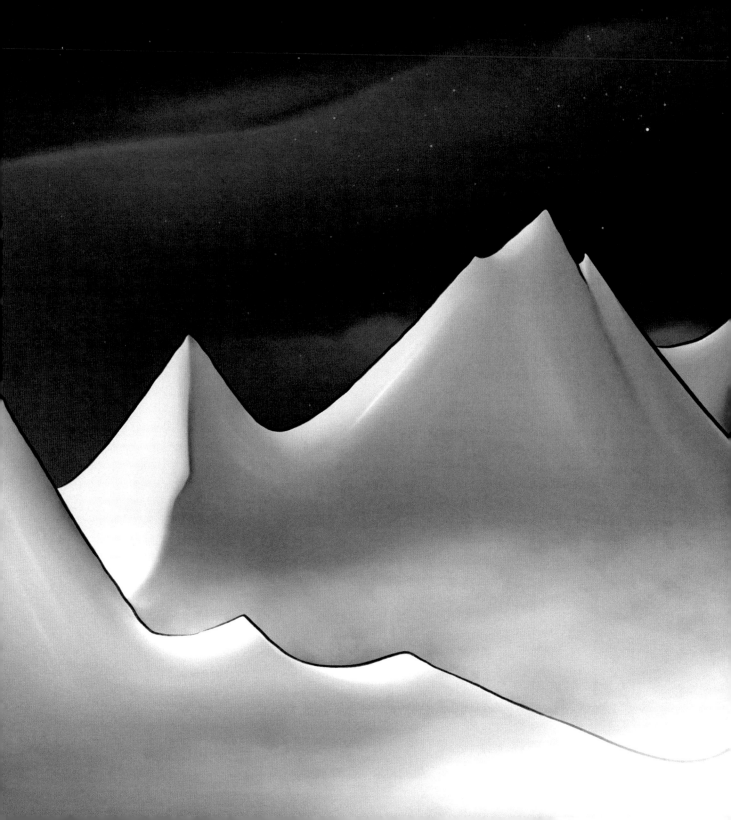

Made in the USA
Monee, IL
31 October 2024

69064109R00024